To my daughters, Krise and Kyle,
a constant source of inspiration.

One

TRACY bounced on the skinniest branch of the walnut tree in her front yard. The heels of her muddy tennis shoes kicked impatiently at the tree's bark. Then she glanced at her digital watch. Another thirty seconds had blinked off. She rolled a glob of gum into a ball and shoved it into one of the tree's knots.

"Aren't you finished, yet?" she huffed impatiently.

Jill pushed her licorice-colored bangs to the side and steadied herself with locked ankles. She leaned back to admire the freshly carved initials. "Yup," she said proudly. "A work of art!"

Tracy strained her neck trying to see the

letters but *J.M. loves* was all she could make out. Big deal. She knew that *J.M.* stood for Jill Mathews. After all, they'd been best friends since the first grade. It was the two other initials that she was dying to see.

Jill covered the bottom half of the carving with her hand. "No fair," she said. "You have to carve yours first. Then we'll show them together. That was the deal."

"Yeah, yeah." Tracy nodded. "I know."

Tracy held the letter opener (on temporary loan from her sister's desk) by its pearly handle. She carefully etched the first two letters of her name, Tracy Benedict. Then her thoughts drifted dreamily to *R.A.*, the second half of the inscription. *R.A.* was the cutest thing Tracy had ever seen. He had a deep tan, sun-bleached hair, and chocolate brown eyes. Tracy wasn't sure if his curly hair was natural or one of those perms. And who cared? Just thinking about him gave her goose bumps!

"All finished," Tracy said, blowing the sawdust

out of *R.A.* She wiped the letter opener on her bleach-stained sweatshirt. "Turn around and we'll switch branches. Then I'll count to three and we'll turn back at the same time." Tracy giggled. "I bet you'll never guess what my initials are!"

For an instant Tracy and Jill were suspended between the branches. The leaves brushed against the roof of Tracy's house with a swishing sound. A dozen or so sticky walnuts toppled from the branches. They both stopped and shushed each other. If Tracy got caught climbing the old walnut tree, she'd spend another weekend cleaning the walnuts and their stains off the front patio. Otherwise the mess could be blamed on squirrels.

"Hide your eyes," Tracy said, covering her face. She eyed Jill through the cracks between her fingers to make sure she wasn't peeking. "On the count of three, ready? One, two, three!"

Tracy dropped her hand and stared wide-eyed at Jill's initials. Her mouth fell open, so open, in fact, that if her rubber bands weren't holding her braces in place her jaw would've touched her chest.

"Who is *R.A.*?" Tracy demanded.

"That's what I'd like to know!" Jill replied.

"I asked you first." Tracy fumed. "Besides, I *saw* him first."

Tracy would never forget the first time she laid eyes on Richard Arnold. It was the last day of school, and she was cleaning out her desk. The door opened, and in walked the fifth-grade teacher who'd be taking over in the fall. Tracy was so flustered that she knocked her notebook to the floor. Paper scattered everywhere. Mr. Arnold knelt to help Tracy pick up the papers and their eyes locked. It was love at first sight.

"How do you know you'll even get him for a teacher?" Jill asked. "There are three fifth-grade classes."

It never occured to Tracy that she *wouldn't* be in Mr. Arnold's room. "We'll just have to figure out a way," she said. Being in Mr. Arnold's room would make the difference between liking school and hating it. She'd even put up with the fifth-grade science fair if Mr. Arnold was her teacher.

Tracy was quiet when she was wearing her thinking cap. The late summer sun glistened on the styling gel she used to keep her baby fine hair slicked into place. Tracy hated the color of her hair. It wasn't blonde. But it wasn't brown, either. It reminded her of the crusty jack cheese on her mother's burnt enchiladas.

"I got it!" Tracy said. "Summer school lasts for another week. We'll ride our bikes to school and ask Mr. Arnold if we're in his class."

Tracy used her tongue to unhook a rubber band from her new braces. It flew out of her mouth hitting the *R.A.* initials with a bull's-eye aim, as if she was adding an exclamation point to her statement.

Jill and Tracy were shaking hands on the brainstorm when a yellow Volkswagen bug gunned its engine. Tracy looked down as the "banana" bounced up the driveway. It was

Tracy's older sister, Kristina. If she spotted them in the tree she'd snitch for sure. She'd been waiting for a chance to get even with Tracy for hiding her retainer in the sugar bowl.

Tracy spun around and faced Jill, making a gag motion with her finger. She then stretched her arms around the tree trunk. The bark scratched her cheek. Both girls closed their eyes and held their breaths. The only sound came from Kristina who was rustling through packages in her car.

"MOM!" Kristina yelled. "Come quick!"

Tracy opened one eye long enough to see her sister standing on the welcome mat. She had a brown grocery bag under each arm, plus one hanging on her wrist. She was nudging the door with her foot when it opened.

"Kristina," Tracy heard her mother's voice say. "Let me give you a hand." They went inside.

There was a loud sigh when Tracy finally exhaled. "Let's get down from here," she whispered.

Too bad the walnut tree was off-limits. Her

11

mom didn't mind if Tracy climbed the other trees in the backyard. But none of those trees had good carving bark like the walnut tree.

Tracy swung a leg over the branch. She balanced on her stomach and felt around for the top step. It was a two-by-four nailed to the tree trunk. Then the letter opener slipped out of her pocket and toppled to the ground. Tracy gasped as the mother-of-pearl handle smashed into a million pieces. She quickly shot Jill a glance of *now we've had it!*

"What was that?" Kristina could be heard from inside. Then a shrill "MOTHER!" tested the sound barrier.

Mrs. Benedict followed her oldest daughter to the front patio. "Tracy?" she asked, standing under the tree. All Tracy could see was the top of her dark brown head. "I thought we had an understanding about that tree?"

"The tree!" Kristina screeched. "Who cares about the stupid tree?! Look at what the little monster did to my letter opener!"

Tracy wanted to say that she was sorry, that it was an accident. But Kristina was making so much noise that no one else could get a word in. Instead, Tracy scooted back to her spot on the middle branch. It was safer.

"What do you have to say for yourself, young lady?" her mother asked. Her hands were on her hips and her elbows stuck out like coat hangers.

"I'm sorry, Mom," Tracy said. "Really . . . ."

"*Sorry* isn't going to fix my letter opener." Kristina was steaming. She was on her knees picking up the shiny pieces of the handle. "It's ruined!"

Mom shook her head. "Tracy," she began. "You're going to have to work around the house for your sister." She paused. "Until the debt is paid off."

Tracy couldn't think of anything worse. "Kristina's slave?"

"I want every single one of those walnuts picked up and the patio hosed off," her mother continued. "And you're grounded for a week for taking someone's property without permission."

"A whole week?" Tracy's voice cracked.

That was worse than being her sister's slave. She thought about Mr. Arnold. There was only a week of summer school left. How could she find out about her fifth-grade class assignment now?

Two

TRACY put on a pair of rubber gloves and opened her sister's drawer in the bathroom. It was the biggest mess she'd ever seen. There were a half-dozen tubes of lipstick with missing caps. A tangled wad of lemon blonde hair was stuck to a dried glob of toothpaste. Tracy considered squirting glue in the drawer to close it permanently. Just then, her sister popped in.

Kristina bent to smooth her leg warmers over her sweats. A pair of tennis shoes were knotted over her shoulder. "How's it going?"

"Someone should declare this spot a disaster area," Tracy answered. "Do you really use all of this junk?"

Kristina patted her sister's head. "Be a good kid and maybe you'll inherit it someday."

Tracy scrunched her nose. "No thanks."

The only thing Tracy wanted to inherit from her sister was her electric razor. She hated the hair on her legs. It was long and stuck out like barbed wire. She wasn't allowed to shave until she started junior high school. That's why she plastered her legs with cream—to smash the hair down.

Then there were her sister's brains. She wouldn't mind having a little of them, too. Tracy got all *C's* on her last report card, except for the B^+ in physical education. Big deal. It didn't impress anyone. Especially her parents who kept telling her that she didn't try hard enough.

"When you're done with the bathroom . . . " Kristina paused to tie her long blonde hair in a ponytail with a multicolored headband, "there's a ton of ironing in the laundry room."

Tracy slammed the drawer. "You never told me how much I owe for the letter opener. How am I supposed to know when it's paid off?"

"Because I'll tell you."

"That's not fair," Tracy said angrily. She snapped the tip of one glove and it snapped back. "Ouch!"

"You should've thought of that *before* you went shoplifting in my bedroom."

Tracy knew her sister bought the letter opener at a fraternity garage sale. Kristina was a freshman studying computer science at the local college. At least that's what she said she was studying. Tracy thought she spent more time studying boys.

"Mom's dropping me off at the gym," Kristina said. "And don't use starch on my shirts."

"Yeah, yeah." Tracy nudged the door shut with her knee.

Tracy opened a compact and covered her nose with a thick layer of face powder. If she wanted to look pretty enough to attract Mr. Arnold, she'd have to hide her freckles. They made her look her age, not that age was a problem. There were lots of women who were dating older men. Tracy could think of five or six of them on her mom's soap operas.

The doorbell rang, and Tracy thought she was hearing wedding bells. "Oh, Mr. Arnold," she sighed. "We'd make a perfect couple!"

A loud *knock, knock, knock* snapped Tracy out of her trance. "Coming!" she yelled.

Jill stood at the front door. "I saw your sister and mom leave," she said. "Your dad isn't home, is he?"

"Nah, he's still off on that business trip. Come in."

"Is it okay?" Jill asked, "even though you're grounded?"

"They never said I couldn't have someone over." Tracy led the way to the kitchen. "Besides, I'm starving. Even real-life prisoners get bread and water."

Tracy opened the refrigerator door. She pushed the yogurt to one side, choosing the flour tortillas and cheddar cheese. The margarine was in a dish on the counter. It was real mushy, just the way she liked it.

"I know how we can find out if *R.A.* is our fifth-grade teacher," Jill said.

Tracy tore a tortilla down the middle. She handed half to Jill. She then folded the other half into a triangle and shoved it into her mouth. "How?" she asked, chomping.

Jill dragged her half of the tortilla over the margarine. "We'll call the school and ask him."

"*We'll* call the school?" Tracy had never called a school in her life. "Who's we?"

"I don't know." Jill shrugged. "How about your sister? Her voice sounds old."

Tracy shook her head. "I'd rather eat slugs than ask her for a favor."

Jill stared at the snaillike trail of butter on her tortilla. "Yuck!"

Tracy sliced the cheddar cheese and put it on two tortillas. She then went to the pantry for a can of black olives. She grabbed the one labeled pitted and put it in the electric can opener. Tracy knew Jill was keeping quiet to let her brainstorm the problem. There was something about fixing food that made Tracy's creative juices flow.

"We'll flip to see who calls," Tracy finally said. "Do you have any change?"

Jill dug into her pocket and turned it inside out. A quarter slipped through her fingers and fell on the floor. It spun on its side. Tracy flattened it with her bare foot.

"Whose head is on the quarter?" Tracy asked.

"That's easy," Jill answered, grinning. "George Washington."

Tracy lifted her foot to reveal the tail-side of the quarter. "Wrong," she said. "It's an eagle."

"You tricked me!" Jill stomped on the kitchen linoleum.

"Okay, okay. I'll make the call. But if things get messed up, don't blame me."

Tracy sat on a stool at the kitchen counter. She opened the family address book to the *P* page. Francis Parkman Elementary School was the first entry. The telephone receiver felt like one of her sister's barbells. It seemed as if it was too heavy to pick up.

"Come on, Tracy," Jill said. "Quit stalling."

"I'm not stalling," she lied. "I'm thinking of what to say."

What was she going to say? "Hello, Mr. Arnold? This is Tracy Benedict. You don't know me very well, but I'm going to marry you someday"? What if the principal answered? Oh, no, what a thought!

Tracy eyed the square buttons on the phone. They were just waiting to be pushed. She lifted the receiver and held it to her ear. The dial tone was one of the most obnoxious noises ever invented. Tracy wondered who invented it. Who invented the dial tone? It sounded like a question from a trivia game. Tracy often let her mind wander when she didn't want to do something. Finally, she punched the school's number.

Tracy chewed on the only nail that was longer than the end of her finger. Then she bit it off and spit it out. Jill hopped up on the counter. She planted both of her feet on a stool. She wrapped her arms around her knees and hugged them to her chest. If someone had dropped a pin, they both would've had heart attacks.

"Who's this?" Tracy sounded surprised. She put her hand over the mouthpiece and whispered to Jill. "It's the secretary."

Jill nodded for her to go on.

"May I please speak to Mr. Arnold?" She was using her best telephone manners. Then her voice squeaked, "What do you mean he's not there? Oh, I see. Okay. Thanks." Tracy hung up and turned to Jill. "He's not teaching summer school." Tracy shook her head. "Why can't we call him at home?"

"What's this *we* business?" Jill asked.

"Hey, I made the first call, didn't I? Now it's your turn."

Jill jumped off the counter and headed for the tortillas. "I'm not supposed to talk with my mouth full." Then she added, "What happens if I'm in his class and you're not?"

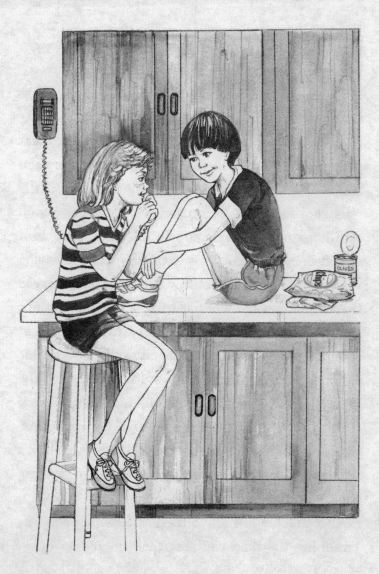

Tracy couldn't believe her ears. "How can you say such a thing?"

Tracy had already outlined the whole fifth-grade year. She had written three rough drafts before she had come up with the final plan. Next to the first Roman numeral *HELPER* was printed in bold letters. That's where she had listed the things she could do to help in the classroom: grade papers, sharpen pencils, clean erasers, etc.

The next category was *ROMANCE*. There she had listed the things she would give Mr. Arnold to make him notice her: a shiny apple on his desk in the morning, chocolate kisses in his lunch at noon, and secret notes in his cubby after school.

Every night she would study, study, study. When Mr. Arnold asked a question, Tracy Benedict would have the answer. And every time Mr. Arnold needed a volunteer, Tracy Benedict's hand would shoot in the air. She had everything figured out.

"I can't believe all of the Arnolds." Tracy was scanning the pages of the thick telephone book.

"And look at all the *R* Arnolds. There must be a dozen of them!"

"How are we going to find out which one is our *R.A.*?" Jill asked.

Tracy shoved the phone across the counter to Jill. "We'll call and ask."

"All of them?"

"I don't know what else to do." Tracy punched the numbers of the first R. Arnold and handed the receiver to Jill. "Come on, there's nothing to it."

Jill pushed her wedged-cut hair behind one ear. "It's ringing," she said. "Maybe I'll luck out and nobody'll be home."

Jill was sitting four or five feet away. Tracy could hear a man's voice. "Hello?" he answered. Jill didn't move a muscle, not even a flutter of her eyelashes. She was scared stiff. The voice repeated, "Hello? Hello?"

Jill slammed down the receiver.

"You act like you've never used a telephone before," Tracy said. Then she redialed. "Watch a real pro in action."

The same man's voice answered. This time he said, "If you don't stop playing with the phone I'll report you to the telephone company!"

This time Tracy slammed down the receiver. "Did you hear what he said?"

Jill didn't have time to answer. The phone rang. "He had it traced!" Jill said.

Tracy stared wide-eyed. "How could he do that?"

"I don't know." Jill shook her head. "But they do it all the time on TV."

"What if it's my mom?" Tracy asked. "If I don't answer she'll think I'm out playing."

"Then answer it."

Tracy snatched the receiver. "Hello?"

It was a man's voice.

Three

TRACY was happy when the man's voice turned out to be her dad's. Not just because it meant the phone hadn't been traced, but because it seemed like forever since she'd talked to him. He was in Japan selling computer gizmos for his company.

He called to say he'd be home in a week, and that had been a week ago. Their house had been buzzing with activity ever since. Tracy was in charge of the welcome home banner. She bought a ten-foot-long strip of white paper from the butcher shop and colored it with the brightest poster paint she could find.

Her mom was making her homemade spaghetti

with her special sauce. That's what her dad craved most when he was traveling in a foreign country. Pizza was planned for the second night. Tracy's favorite meals were spaghetti and pizza, too. Unfortunately, they were the only two things Tracy had in common with her dad.

"Tracy?" her mom yelled from the kitchen. "I could use some help out here."

Tracy bounced into the kitchen just in time to see her mom shove dough into the mouth of the pasta machine. Mrs. Benedict used one hand to sprinkle the dough with flour so the wormlike strands wouldn't stick together. With her other hand she used the spatula to cut the spaghetti into 12-inch-long pieces.

"I need help pulling the spaghetti apart," her mom said. "And we have to find a place to hang it."

Tracy grabbed a ball of twine from the laundry room. She tied one end to the refrigerator. She wove the other end through the oven door handle and knotted it on the pantry knob. The kitchen looked like the giant spider's web at her school's Halloween carnival last year.

"I have two reasons to celebrate today," Tracy said. She untangled the curls of dough and hung them over the twine. "Dad's coming home and I'm off restriction."

"And you paid your sister back," her mother added.

"I did?!"

"Yup." Her mom nodded. "I decided the letter opener was worth a dollar seventy-five."

"Wow! That's super. Thanks, Mom."

Tracy rated the past week with the Fourth of July. It hadn't been as good as Easter or Christmas vacations. After all, she had been grounded. But it had been fun getting ready for her dad. Kristina had only called her a nerd once. She had let Tracy put the crisscrosses on her peanut butter cookies *and* lick the bowl. Tracy didn't even have to wash the cookie sheets.

Kristina bounced into the kitchen looking like an outer-space alien. A mask of gooey green stuff was hardening on her face. It cracked when she talked. "A taxi just pulled up," she said, trying not to move her lips. "I think it's Daddy."

Mrs. Benedict glanced at the clock on the stove. "That's impossible. He's not even due at the airport for another two hours."

"Mo-om." Kristina gave the word two syllables. "Don't you think I know my own father?"

Her mom's eyes filled with tears. "Look at me," she said, wiping her hands on a dish towel. "I'm a mess."

"You're a mess?" Kristina was yanking electric curlers out of her hair. "Look at me!"

Tracy tossed the last strand of spaghetti over the twine. She then made a beeline through the living room and out the front door. She raced down the steps squealing. "Daddy! Daddy! You're home!"

Mr. Benedict was helping the taxi driver drag a heavy suitcase from the backseat. When he saw Tracy he knelt with open arms. "Peanuts!" he said. "If you're not a sight for sore eyes!"

Her father called her "Peanuts" because she had only weighed five-and-a-half pounds when she was born. She was still the shortest kid in her class. Her mom said there was nothing wrong with a girl being petite. But Tracy was tired of all the shrimp jokes. "When it rains Tracy's the last one to know." "How's the weather down there?" She'd heard them all.

"I'm so glad you're home!" Tracy said through watery eyes. She squeezed her dad so hard she thought he'd pop. "I didn't think I'd ever see you again!"

"I know what you mean," her dad said. He returned the hug with equal force. "Six weeks is too long to be away."

"Daddy!" Kristina had washed the mask off her face and pulled all of the rollers out of her hair. But her hair wasn't brushed out. The blonde curls bounced against her shoulders like little springs.

"How's my favorite brain child?" Mr. Benedict hugged Kristina. "Are you still planning to be the first woman president?"

"Oh, Daddy." Kristina blushed.

Mrs. Benedict stepped outside, onto the front porch. She was the best crier Tracy had ever heard. It sounded like something was stuck in her windpipe. When she wiped her eyes with the kitchen towel, flour streaked across her cheeks. "Ken!" she said between sobs.

Mr. Benedict rushed to the porch. He scooped Mrs. Benedict in his arms and swung her in a circle. Her apron ballooned in slow motion. "Linda!" he said.

"Ken!" her mom repeated.

The scene reminded Tracy of an old movie. The only things missing were a rack of candy bars and hot buttered popcorn.

"Ken, when did you grow the mustache?" Mrs. Benedict asked.

Tracy thought something about her dad was different. She hadn't quite figured out what it was. The mustache was the same spun gold color as his hair. It made his dark brown eyes look even

33

darker. "So that's what was tickling my ear!" She laughed.

Her parents sputtered gushy things in each other's ears. Then they giggled like a couple of school kids. Tracy knew she was lucky to have both of her biological parents. Jill's parents were divorced. When her mom remarried Jill got custody of a bratty little stepbrother.

Tracy decided the reason that her parents got along so well was because her dad was twelve years older than her mom. There was just enough of an age difference to keep things interesting. And not enough that there was a generation gap. Just like me and *R.A.*

"Did you bring me anything?" Tracy asked.

"Did I bring you anything?" her dad teased. "Let's go inside. I can't wait to taste your mom's spaghetti sauce."

Her mom pointed to Tracy's welcome home banner. "See what Tracy made?"

Her dad brushed his fingers through Tracy's hair. "Thanks, Peanuts."

Tracy stood between her mom and dad and wrapped her arms around their waists. Kristina was on the other side of Mr. Benedict. They looked like a chorus line as they edged sideways through the front door. "One, two, three, kick," Tracy said.

Mr. Benedict twirled the combination lock on his suitcase and popped the latch. Tracy scooted in for a closer look. The case wasn't filled with the usual junk. Instead, there were little bundles wrapped in newspaper and tied with string. He handed the biggest package to Mrs. Benedict.

"You didn't have to bring me anything," her mom said. "But I'm sure glad you did!"

She snapped the string and tore open the paper. Another piece of newspaper was wrapped inside. Then another and another. Finally, she got down to the last layer. The package was the size of a hard-boiled egg. She carefully slipped her fingernail under the last piece of tape. A jade ring tumbled out. It was in a gold setting surrounded by little diamonds.

"Oh, my goodness!" her mother gasped. "It's the most beautiful thing I've ever seen!"

"It's hard to believe what I'll go through for a plate of spaghetti," her dad joked.

Kristina's turn was next. She didn't waste any time ripping open the newspaper. "Wow!" she exclaimed. Her gift was a pair of jade earrings. "They're really *bad!*"

"That means good," her mom explained.

Mr. Benedict nodded. "Okay, Peanuts," he said. "It's your turn. Are you ready?"

Tracy closed her eyes and held out her hand. "Ready!"

Four

TRACY flopped on her bed. She buried her head in her pillow trying to muffle her sobs. She couldn't remember the last time she had been so excited about getting a present, unless it was last Christmas when the bike appeared wrapped in a sheet under the tree.

She also couldn't remember when she was more disappointed in what she got. Except the year the tags got mixed up. Tracy ended up with her grandma's hot water bottle. It was the hardest thank you note she ever had to write.

Tracy thought it was about time there was something besides plastic in her jewelry box. All of her jewelry was dress-up stuff she'd rescued from the sale bin at the dime store. She also thought she was old enough to have something dainty around her neck. It didn't have to be expensive as long as it was real.

That's why Tracy burst into tears when she opened her present. She couldn't believe that her dad would give her a calculator. Who cares that it was a Japanese calculator? You could buy those anywhere. Her mom got a personal gift and so did Kristina. Tracy's calculator was about as personal as a pair of wool socks.

Tracy spent the welcome home dinner locked in her bedroom. Her mom came to the door and tried to cheer her up. Kristina even tried a string of elephant jokes. There was only one person she wanted to come to her door. And he didn't come until after dinner.

"Open the door, Peanuts," her dad said. "Please?"

Tracy sat upon her bed. She was surrounded by wads of crumpled tissues. The empty box was upside down on the floor. "It's open," she answered between sniffles.

Her dad came in and quietly sat on the edge of the bed. He didn't say anything at first. It was as if he knew what he wanted to say but didn't know where to start.

"I don't understand why you're upset," her dad finally began. He took his handkerchief out of his pocket and wiped Tracy's tears. "I thought you'd like the calculator."

Tracy hugged her pillow. "I do like it, Dad. It's just that . . . . Why didn't I get jewelry like Mom and Kristina?"

"Because I thought you'd like a more practical gift. Something to help you in school." Her dad picked up the calculator from the top of Tracy's dresser. "This isn't an ordinary calculator," he said. "It has all the latest features. The stores don't even stock them yet."

Tracy scooted closer. "Really?"

He flipped the ON switch. "Look at the display panel. Have you ever seen one that lights up like that? And it has a special memory function."

Tracy leaned in for a closer look. "I'll be able to check my answers in math, huh?"

"It might help in the science fair, too," he added. "I remember when Kristina was in fifth grade. Her project won a blue ribbon."

Tracy was sorry she didn't have an *A* on her last report card. Even her *B*+ in gym was lost against Kristina's straight *A's*.

"You're not stupid, Tracy," he added. "With a little effort you could bring all your grades up."

"I do try," Tracy said. "It's just that . . . ."

"Come on, now, Peanuts. No excuses." He put his arm around Tracy's shoulder and gave a gentle squeeze. "I know you can do better."

Tracy promised to do better every time they had one of these heart-to-heart talks. She meant it, too. She wanted her parents to be as proud of her as they were of Kristina. But there was always something more exciting to do than study.

Her dad kissed Tracy and they said good night. He stopped at the door before turning out the light. "I'm sorry if I hurt your feelings, Peanuts," he said. "I guess I don't think of you as being old enough for jewelry. You're still my little girl . . . my *peanut.* Am I forgiven?"

"Uh-huh." Tracy nodded. "I love you, Daddy."

"I love you, too." He switched off the light and closed the door.

Tracy fell asleep wondering if Kristina had inherited all of the brain genes. Maybe they were used up when it was time for Tracy to be born. Or maybe she was adopted and her real parents were not too smart. Even her dreams turned into nightmares. One minute her dad was her dad, then *poof!* There was Mr. Arnold.

*　*　*　*　*

Mrs. Benedict was in the kitchen pouring milk over her cereal. She had just washed her hair, and her permanent made wet ringlets. When it dried, she'd fluff it out with a pick. Then it would hang down to her shoulders. Except for the crackle of the cereal in her bowl, everything in the house was quiet.

"Where is everybody?" Tracy asked.

"Down at the computer lab," her mom said. "Your dad's helping Kristina with her program."

Tracy was disappointed. She thought her dad would be helping her with her new calculator this morning. Instead, he was with Kristina. Tracy took a bowl out of the cupboard and sat down next to her mom. "Am I adopted?" she asked.

The question took her mom by surprise. "What in the world would make you ask a question like that?"

It wasn't an easy thing for Tracy to say. "Because sometimes I think Daddy likes Kristina better than he does me."

"Tracy," her mom said, shocked. "How can you say such a thing?"

"Because he's always comparing me to her," Tracy said sadly. She popped a handful of dry cereal into her mouth and crunched loudly. "And he hardly said anything about my banner. If Kristina had spent three hours painting welcome home he would've gushed all over the place."

"Tracy." Her mom's voice pitched. "What's gotten into you?"

Once Tracy got started she had a hard time stopping. "Kristina this. Kristina that," she whined. "Why can't he accept me the way I am?"

"Your father loves you very much," her mother said. "And he does the best he can to show it."

"He doesn't have any trouble showing Kristina."

"That's different." Her mom paused. "They have more in common."

"Like brains?"

"You have brains, too, Tracy. Your dad would just like to see you use them."

It was the same old story—an instant replay of last night's lecture. Sometimes Tracy wondered if getting A's would even make a difference. What if her father found another excuse for treating her like the second banana?

Mrs. Benedict decided it was time to change the subject. "I want you to pick up a few things at the grocery store," she said. "You'll have to put the basket on your bike."

"Great idea." Tracy had been cooped up in the house for a week. "I'll call Jill."

The center of town was only a ten-minute bike ride away. After calling Jill, Tracy put the bowls in the dishwasher. She headed for the garage. She swung one leg over the sheepskin bike seat and coasted down the driveway. "Freedom!" she yipped.

Jill was waiting on the corner of Vine and Spring streets. "Boy, am I glad to see you," she said. "This has been the most boring week!"

Tracy's rear tire skidded a black stripe on the sidewalk. "Our house wasn't boring," she said. "It was a mad house. Did I tell you my dad came home?"

"Really?" Jill asked excitedly. "What did he bring you?"

Tracy wished there was a way to say "calculator" to make it sound exciting. "A calculator," she said. "Wait'll you see it. It does

all kinds of things."

"It sounds boring to me."

The grocery store was only three blocks down the street. They walked their bikes and yacked along the way. Tracy had been so busy with the homecoming plans that she hadn't even had time to talk on the phone. Jill had lots of news. Her stepbrother had frozen her toothbrush in a tray of ice cubes.

"Have you ever tried to brush your teeth with a popsicle?" Jill asked.

They reached the store and pushed their bikes into the rack. Jill strapped them together with the chain of her combination lock. Tracy reached into her pocket and pulled out the grocery list.

"Water chestnuts and smoked oysters?" She stomped on the rubber mat. The automatic door swung open. "Have you ever heard of anything so gross?"

"Yuck!" Jill agreed.

They tested several carts before they found one without a wobbly wheel. They went up one aisle and down another. Jill was the driver. Tracy toppled a can off the shelf and backhanded it into the cart. The can of tomato juice was a slam-dunk. Tracy was searching for the water-packed tuna when Jill grabbed her T-shirt. She stretched the corner until it was a foot longer than the rest.

Tracy pulled loose. "What's the matter?"

Jill's jaw dropped open. Her large dark eyes grew even larger. Her lips moved but nothing came out. Then "yu-yu-yu" rolled off the tip of her tongue. It didn't sound like anything in the English language.

"Is it animal, vegetable, or mineral?" Tracy coaxed.

"It's Mr. Arnold!" Jill finally said. "He just went down the bakery aisle!"

Five

TRACY stretched her neck to peek around a display of hot dog buns. Mr. Arnold was reading the ingredients on the package of wheat bread. He was wearing a well-worn pair of tennis shoes, a T-shirt with printing about some marathon, and a pair of running shorts.

"Look at those legs!" Tracy said. She tossed three packages of hot dog buns into her cart so she could see better. "I can't believe he's grocery shopping, just like a real person."

Jill removed another three packages and made her own viewing tunnel. "Like a real *unmarried* person."

"I hope you won't be too disappointed when he

49

falls for me," Tracy said. "Hey, I have an idea. You can be my maid-of-honor."

"Don't count your chickens, Tracy Benedict."

Mr. Arnold traded the first loaf of bread for one labeled all-natural.

"He reminds me of someone," Jill said, puzzled. "But I don't know who it is."

Tracy scratched her head. "Yeah, he does look like someone." Then she dismissed the thought. "Mom says you can tell a lot about a person by what they put in their cart." She eyeballed Mr. Arnold's cart carefully. Maybe someday she'd be doing the shopping for him. "Granola bars and sparkling cider. Look at all of the fruits and vegetables. No wonder he looks so good."

"Oh, my gosh!" Jill stammered. "He-he-he's coming this way!"

"Oh, no!" Tracy howled. "Look at me! I'm a disaster!"

Tracy was wearing the red T-shirt that got mixed up in the load of white wash. It was covered with bleach splotches. And without styling gel, her mousy brown bangs hung in her eyes. At least she'd remembered to brush her teeth. There was nothing worse than looking at cereal stuck in someone's braces.

"This way!" Tracy said. She spun the cart in a semicircle. "Maybe he won't see us!"

Jill grabbed the cart and it screeched to a stop. "No. This is the chance we've been waiting for! You can ask Mr. Arnold about our class assignment."

"I can't let him see me like this!" Tracy said. She tried to stuff her T-shirt into her jeans, but the material bulged around her waist. It looked like she had a potbelly. She pulled the T-shirt out and smoothed the wrinkles. "How do I look now?"

"You look fine," Jill said.

Tracy didn't think she sounded very convincing. "What about my hair?" she asked.

Tracy looked for a display of mirrors, but the beauty and cosmetic aisle was at the other end of the store. Instead, she picked up a jar of pickles.

She turned the label sideways and stared at her reflection. It was as though she was looking into a fish bowl. Her face was short and fat and her eyes were popping out of their sockets.

"I'm getting out of here!" Tracy slammed the pickles into the cart.

"Oh, no you don't!" Jill said. She hooked her finger through the loop of Tracy's jeans.

Tracy tried to get away. Her feet made a running motion, but she wasn't going anywhere. That's the crummy thing about being a shrimp. Everyone is bigger than you are.

Then a deep voice said, "Hello, girls. How's your summer going?"

Jill's dark eyes grew wide. "Uh-uh-uh . . . ."

Tracy spun one-hundred-and-eighty degrees. She was hoping that Mr. Arnold wouldn't recognize her from behind. A display of panty hose in plastic egg-shaped containers stared her in the face. The models hardly had any clothes on. Tracy's face reddened with a stinging flush.

"Are you having a party?" Mr. Arnold asked.

Tracy turned around and her mouth dropped open. The rubber bands on her braces made her jaw feel like a drawbridge. She stared at the smile on Mr. Arnold's tanned face. His sun-bleached eyelashes made his dark brown eyes look like two pieces of coal. Tracy thought he looked more like a movie star than a fifth-grade teacher.

"A party?" Tracy squeaked. Her head felt as if it was full of cotton candy. She grabbed onto the cart and steadied herself so she wouldn't faint.

Mr. Arnold pointed to all the packages of hot dog buns in Tracy's cart. "Looks like a wienie roast," he said.

"Yeah." Tracy agreed. She didn't know what else to say.

"See you both in a couple of weeks," Mr. Arnold said and headed to the check-out line.

Tracy nodded numbly.

The girls huddled together, then burst into the giggles. Tracy poked Jill's rib cage and said, "Shhhhh!" Then they giggled even louder. Jill was hunched over the cart when Tracy gave it a sharp push. Jill doubled in half and fell in.

"What do you think you're doing?" Jill gasped. She was kicking her feet trying to get her balance.

Tracy didn't give her a chance to climb out. She pushed the cart as fast as she could down the aisle. "Paying you back," she laughed, "for grabbing onto my pants."

"If we don't stop acting like nerds . . . ," Jill screeched. She was hanging on for dear life. "Mr. Arnold will make sure we're *not* in his class."

Tracy spun the cart and headed back to the hot dog bun display. "Okay, let's restack the buns. There's only two things left on my list. You get the tuna fish and I'll get the shaving cream."

Jill counted the number of things in the cart. "I'll meet you at the quick-check." She took off for the canned goods aisle.

Tracy sped across the store to the aisle with shaving cream. She eyed the different kinds. There were cans of lime, lemon, and spearmint. Some were foamy and others were gel. The list didn't say what kind to buy. She grabbed the can that promised a closer shave without irritation.

Tracy zigzagged around the other shoppers to the quick-check line. She tossed her groceries on the counter and kept an eye out for Jill. That's when she saw Mr. Arnold pushing his cart through the double doors. She dug the folded ten-dollar bill out of her pocket and handed it to the checker.

"Tuna fish is coming," Tracy said. "She'll take the change." She pointed to Jill with her thumb.

"Wait a minute . . . " the lady started to say. But it was too late. Tracy had left her groceries on the counter and was out the door.

Tracy sneaked through the parking lot hiding behind cars. The asphalt was so hot it burned through her tennis shoes. Sweat dripped down her forehead. Then she saw Mr. Arnold. He was filling the trunk of his sportscar with bags of groceries. Tracy hid behind a pickup truck parked across from his car.

Then a booming "TRACY!" threatened to shatter the sound barrier.

Mr. Arnold turned around. Tracy dropped behind a white sidewall tire.

"TRACY!" Jill's voice repeated even more

loudly. "Where are you?"

Tracy shuddered. She closed her eyes and put her hands over her ears. She was sending Jill shut up vibrations. It didn't work. Jill came whizzing by on her bike shouting louder than ever. Then she spotted Tracy.

"What are you doing?!" Jill howled. The groceries teetered in the basket. "I've been looking all over for you!"

Tracy put her finger to her mouth. "Shhhh!" Then she pointed to Mr. Arnold. He was climbing into the front seat of his car. Tracy stood up when he slammed the door. "We have to follow him!"

Tracy ran through the parking lot. She jumped on her bike and bounced the front tire out of the rack. Jill had already taken off down the street. Fortunately, there was lots of traffic and Mr. Arnold was bumper-to-bumper all the way down Spring Street. By the time he reached the first stop sign, Tracy had caught up to Jill.

"I hope he doesn't live very far away." Jill

huffed out of breath. "If I'm late for lunch my mom'll have a fit."

Tracy's situation was worse. The tuna fish in the bag was for her dad's lunch. Sometimes he was grumpy if his lunch wasn't ready on time.

Jill pointed to the blinking taillights. "He's turning right."

"Follow that car!" Tracy said, sounding like someone out of a detective movie.

Mr. Arnold rounded the corner and backed into the driveway of a small, neat house. The door on the garage opened automatically. Then the trunk of his car flew open. Mr. Arnold lifted two bags out of the trunk. He then disappeared into the door connecting the garage to the house.

Tracy skidded to a halt. "He lives right in the middle of town," she said, giggling. "We couldn't have planned it better if we'd tried."

Jill was paying more attention to what was going on inside of Mr. Arnold's garage than she was to her driving. The rim of her front tire slammed into the curb. Several cans flew out of the grocery bag. They rolled down the driveway. The can of tuna leading the way. It didn't stop until it hit Mr. Arnold's tire.

"Oh, no!" Tracy gasped.

Tracy jumped off her bike and gathered the spilled goods. She examined each item before returning it to the bag. The only thing damaged was the can of tuna. The label was peeling off and it was dented.

"I've gotta go." Tracy switched the grocery bag to her basket. "Maybe we can play detective after lunch."

"Okay," Jill said, swinging her leg over her bike seat. "See ya."

Tracy hopped on her bike and sped across town. She shifted into a middle gear and pedalled over the bridge that crosses the Salinas river. The cuff of her jeans kept getting caught in the chain. She didn't dare take time to stop and roll it up. She approached the driveway and down-shifted to a coasting speed. She still had one leg dangling over the seat when her dad walked out of the house.

"So there you are," he said. "I hope you have a good excuse for being late."

Six

*I*T *isn't fair!* Tracy thought that should be the title of her diary. Kristina didn't get into trouble when she came home late from a date. She didn't even get caught because everybody was asleep. But when Tracy was half-an-hour late for lunch, LOOK OUT!

Tracy wheeled her bike into the garage. Then she followed her dad into the kitchen. "What time is it?" she asked.

"It's one-thirty," her dad said.

Her mother was waiting inside the kitchen. "What took you so long?"

Kristina had her hand in a bag of barbecued potato chips. "I'm starving to death!"

"We're waiting for an answer," her mom said.

"And I'm waiting for the tuna," Kristina added.

Tracy plopped the grocery bag on the counter. She knew she'd better have a good excuse. To stall for time, she buzzed open the tuna, scooped it into a bowl, and tossed the can in the trash compactor.

"The store was crowded," Tracy said. "And there was a lot of traffic."

Her dad seemed to expect more. "And?" he asked.

"I was talking to Jill and forgot the time." She tried her saddest expression. "I'm sorry."

"You seem to be sorry a lot lately," he said.

Oh, no. He must've heard about Kristina's letter opener. Tracy wished she could go back to the first minutes of his arrival. He was so glad to see her. And that hug! It was the best ever.

"Do you know the definition of responsibility?" he asked.

Tracy had a lump in her throat. She nodded. "Yeah."

"Yes," her dad stressed.

Tracy made the correction. "Yes, Daddy."

Responsibility was discussed over tuna on toasted sourdough. Tracy listened while her dad read the definition out of the dictionary. She tried to use her best table manners. No elbows on the table. Chew with your mouth closed. She even tried to keep her napkin in one piece. It usually ended up on the floor in shreds.

Tracy cleared the dishes after lunch and went to her room. She doodled RESPONSIBILITY across the top of a sheet of notebook paper. The dictionary's definition was, "The state of being responsible." It had been a bonus word on one of last year's spelling tests.

Looking words up in the dictionary reminded Tracy of school. And school reminded her of Mr. Arnold. One thought drifted into another. Soon she was imagining herself in a frilly lace wedding dress. She could even hear the church's organ playing "Here Comes the Bride." She was walking down the aisle with Mr. Arnold. Her father was waiting for her at the altar. Tracy blinked. Something was wrong. Mr. Arnold was in her dad's place and her dad was in Mr. Arnold's place.

"Tracy?" Her father knocked on her door. He popped his head in. "Jill's on the phone."

"Thanks, Dad," Tracy said. She jumped off her bed and raced to the kitchen phone.

"You're not going to believe this!" Jill blurted into the receiver.

"What?" Tracy asked.

"I'm in Mr. Arnold's class!"

Tracy couldn't believe it. "How'd you find out?"

"My mom ran into Mrs. Byrd at the cleaners. And Mrs. Byrd said how happy she was that Mark was going to be in my class. Then she asked my mom if she'd met our new fifth-grade teacher, Mr. Arnold."

"What about me?"

"Geez, Tracy. I wasn't there. This is just what my mom told me."

It wasn't fair that Jill had found out who her teacher was, when Tracy had been dying to know! "I'll talk to you tomorrow." Tracy didn't sound very friendly.

The following day rolled around and Tracy forgot to call Jill. She forgot every day for the next two weeks. And when Jill called she made up an excuse for not coming to the phone. She was mad at Jill for getting into Mr. Arnold's class. Maybe she was a little bit jealous, too.

Tracy rode her bike past Mr. Arnold's house every day, but she never saw him. The day before school started she scratched Jill's initials out of the tree.

The first day of school around the Benedict house was always the same. Tracy changed her clothes three times. She tried the purple dress with the bib collar. Then she tried a simple blouse with a pleated skirt. Everything made her look like a little kid. She finally settled on a new pair of blue jeans. She rolled the cuffs to her knees, fifties-style, like her sister. Then she looked down at her hairy legs. Sighing, she unrolled them back to her ankles.

Tracy banged on the bathroom door. "Can I borrow one of your funky T-shirts?"

Kristina opened the door. She was in the middle of French-braiding her hair. "Why should I let you borrow something of mine?"

"Because it's the first day of school," Tracy pleaded. "And I don't want to look like a nerd."

"Okay," Kristina said. "You can borrow the T-shirt from the summer rock concert."

Tracy threw her arms around Kristina's waist. "You're the best sister!"

Kristina hugged Tracy with her elbows. She was trying not to drop the ends of her French-braid. "Just don't drool on it."

Tracy filled her notebook with paper while she waited for her turn in the bathroom. She wished her hair was long enough to French-braid. It would make her look older. The one time she tried it, all of the little pieces stuck out. Her hair was at an in-between length. The only thing she could do was slick the sides back with styling gel.

"How do I look?" Tracy bounced into the kitchen.

"Very pretty," her dad said. He folded the top on the box of cereal and put the milk in the refrigerator. "Would you like a ride to school?"

"Where's Mom?"

"She's sleeping in this morning."

The Benedicts didn't live far enough out of town to have school bus service. They lived too far for Tracy to walk. She hated to ride her bike to school, especially on the first day. Gnats always got stuck in her styling gel.

Tracy followed her dad to Kristina's banana. Tracy had wanted her sister to name the yellow VW bug a lemon. But Kristina said that was bad luck. It was fun when her mom drove, because she wasn't very good at shifting. Sometimes she'd forget to ease the clutch out and they'd bounce down a whole block. Tracy was glad that her dad was driving. It would give her a chance to have him all to herself.

Mr. Benedict and Tracy buckled their seat belts. As they backed out the driveway, her dad said, "There's something I have to tell you."

Tracy didn't like the sound of her father's voice. "What?"

"Mr. Nerelli called last night."

Tracy knew that a call from her father's boss meant another business trip. "So soon?! But you just got home two weeks ago!"

"I don't want to go either." Her dad's voice was shaky. "But they're having trouble in their Argentine office. And Mr. Nerelli thinks I'm the only one for the job."

"Argentina?" Tracy swallowed hard. There was a huge lump in her throat. "Don't they have bandits down there?"

"No, silly." He eased the banana into the school's loading zone. He set the emergency brake and turned off the ignition. "I know it's been tough on you, Peanuts—me being gone so much." He squeezed Tracy's hand. "But I love you very much."

Now Tracy's voice was shaky. "It's just that I love you so much, Dad. And I miss you when you're gone."

"I know. I know." He understood how Tracy felt. "Maybe someday I'll have a nine-to-five job. Until then we just have to make the best of it."

Tracy kissed him on the cheek. She didn't even care if any of the kids were watching. Then she picked up her lunch and notebook. "I'll see ya later."

"See ya," he said. "And have a *bad* day."

Tracy giggled. It sounded funny when he used one of Kristina's expressions.

"Hey, metal-mouth!" Tracy heard when she slammed the car door. "Whose class are you in?"

Tracy turned around. Steve Weber was standing under the basketball hoop. He jumped up trying to touch the rim. He missed. That's what you get for being such a showoff, Tracy thought.

Tracy shrugged. "I don't know."

Steve brushed the hair out of his eyes. It was

longer than last year. He wore it parted on the side and slicked back. "All the cool kids are in Mrs. Bailey's room," he said.

"What's so cool about a teacher who wears black-and-white saddle shoes?" Tracy stomped. She couldn't stand the thought of getting stuck with Mrs. Bailey. "They went out with the dinosaurs."

Tracy stormed across the playground. She didn't want to waste any more time talking about Mrs. Bailey. Besides, it was getting late. And she wanted to find Jill so that she could apologize *before* she got her class assignment. Otherwise she might get mad again.

Tracy looked in the last stall of the girl's bathroom. It didn't have a door and sometimes Jill liked to swing on the overhead bar. She tried the upper-division drinking fountain and the cinnamon roll line in front of the cafeteria. Then the warning bell rang and the kids raced to their classrooms. They only had five minutes before the tardy bell.

The three fifth-grade classes were in a row across from the kindergarten classrooms. Tacked to the outside of each door was a list of students' names.

Tracy scanned the list on Ms. Miller's door. No Tracy Benedict. "Whew!" She wiped her brow.

The next door would determine Tracy's fate for the next school year. If she was on Mrs. Bailey's list, then she wasn't on Mr. Arnold's. It worked the other way, too. She crossed her fingers and scrunched her toes. Then she stepped in front of Mr. Arnold's door. "In goes the good air, out goes the bad air." She exhaled loudly. "And here goes nothing!"

Seven

TRACY spun around and found herself face-to-face to Mr. Arnold. He looked even better than she'd remembered. His tan was the kind you see on billboards advertising suntan oil. The knot of his tie was loosened around his neck. It was a good thing she'd made that promise to her sister. Otherwise she might've drooled.

"Good morning," Mr. Arnold said.

Tracy felt her cheeks turn the color of a poinsettia. "Good morning."

"Are you in my class?" Mr. Arnold asked.

Tracy opened her mouth, but nothing came out. She shook her head no.

"Maybe next year," Mr. Arnold said before slipping into his classroom.

Next year? Tracy would have to flunk to repeat the fifth grade. And then what guarantee would she have that she'd get his class? No, there was only one thing to do. She had to find another way to get into his classroom.

Tracy walked into Mrs. Bailey's room. She slid into the desk behind Steve Weber. "All right," Steve said. He shook a thumbs-up in her face.

"I'm only staying," Tracy said, "until I can find someone who wants to trade. Otherwise I'm quitting school."

Mrs. Bailey tapped a yardstick on the floor. "Attention," she said. "May I have your attention, please?"

Mrs. Bailey printed her name above the date on the chalkboard. While her back was turned a gooey spitwad splatted the *i*. Tracy tried not to giggle. The wad slid in slow motion into the eraser tray. It wiped out half of September.

"Who's responsible for this?" Mrs. Bailey demanded.

No one made a sound.

"If the person doesn't come forward right this minute—" The veins in Mrs. Bailey's neck stuck out like spaghetti. "There's going to be serious repercussions."

No one moved.

"I'm going to count to three." Mrs. Bailey folded her arms across her chest. "One, two . . . "

That's when the fire alarm went off.

Someone always sets the fire alarm off on the first day of school. It was tradition. It didn't matter if the alarm was planned or not. Everyone still had to march across the playground. Since it was the first day of school they didn't have any instructions on what to do or where to go.

Steve whispered, "Saved by the bell!"

"Stop!" Mrs. Bailey said. But it was too late. Half of the class was out the door.

Tracy joined Mr. Arnold's class on the playground.

"Are you still mad at me?" Jill asked.

"There's nothing to be mad at," Tracy said. "I'm going to be in Mr. Arnold's class by the end of the week."

"How're you going to do that?"

"I'll find a way."

The principal walked across the playground, shouting through a bullhorn. "False alarm. Everyone return to their classes!"

Tracy wasn't in a hurry to go back to Mrs. Bailey's room.

Jill tried to make her feel better. "Mr. Arnold is really hard," she said. "He told us that we have to do a book report every month. And we can't use the same book twice!"

Tracy didn't care if she had to do a book report every day for the rest of her life, if it meant she could be in Mr. Arnold's class.

Steve was tagging behind. "I've got enough money for a couple of cinnamon rolls," he piped in, "if you want something for dessert at lunch."

Tracy stopped in her tracks and Steve almost tripped over her. "Who are you talking to?" she asked.

Steve stared at the little orange basketballs

stamped on his shoelaces. "Both of you," he answered.

Tracy shot him a *don't-be-such-a-nerd* look. She wouldn't be caught dead eating a cinnamon roll with Steve Weber. It would make her feel as if she was two-timing Mr. Arnold.

Tracy and Jill continued to plod along to the fifth-grade classrooms with Steve still a step behind. When they got to Mrs. Bailey's door he opened it for Tracy. But Tracy slipped into Mr. Arnold's room instead.

"What're you doing?" Jill asked.

Tracy didn't answer. She followed Jill to the row of chairs in the back of the class.

Mark Byrd blew a giant grape bubble. It popped and pinkish film covered his nose. "Hey," he said, rubbing the gum into a ball. "You're not supposed to be in this class."

Tracy looked at his pink nose. "Fifth-grade boys are so immature."

Mark answered with a pair of crossed eyes and a wagging tongue.

The door opened and Mr. Arnold appeared. He was taking a head count. Tracy stared at the top of her desk, hoping he wouldn't notice her.

"Twenty-eight," he said. "All present and accounted for. I'm going to send a seating chart around."

Mr. Arnold handed the chart to the first kid in the first row. Tracy giggled nervously. All she had to do was sign her name. Then everything would be official. She watched the chart go up and down each row. It seemed to take forever before it got to her desk.

Tracy leaned across the aisle to Jill. "Can I borrow a pen? All of my junk is in the other room."

"All I have are pencils," Jill answered.

Tracy didn't want to take a chance with a pencil. It could be erased. "Psssst," she said to Mark. "You got a pen?"

Mark was about to pop another bubble when the door opened. Annie Hopkins walked in. She stood at the front of the class with a confused look on her face. "I accidently went to the wrong room," she said.

"I just took a count," Mr. Arnold said. He sat on the corner of his desk. One leg dangled over the edge. "We have the right number."

That's when Mark cleared his throat. It sounded like a lawn mower. "Tracy Benedict isn't supposed to be here," he said.

Everyone turned around and stared at Tracy.

"Tracy?" Mr. Arnold asked. "Would you come to the front of the room, please?"

Tracy tried to stand but the seat of her pants felt as if it was stuck to the chair. She stayed put.

"Aren't you supposed to be in Mrs. Bailey's room?" he asked.

Tracy tried to think of something fast. "I guess I wandered in by mistake after the fire drill," she said. "But as long as I'm here I might as well stay."

Mr. Arnold smiled. "Sorry."

"I can trade with Annie," Tracy said eagerly. "Maybe she'd like to be in Mrs. Bailey's class."

Annie rolled her eyes and made a *tsk* sound. "You gotta be kidding!"

Jill whispered, "He's coming this way."

Sure enough, Mr. Arnold was walking down the center aisle to the back of the room. Tracy couldn't take her eyes off him.

Mr. Arnold held out his hand. "Come on, Tracy," he said. "I'll escort you back."

Eight

BY the time Friday rolled around Tracy was in a state of shock. She'd pleaded with everyone from her parents to the principal. "Please," she'd begged on one knee. "If you put me in Mr. Arnold's room I'll never ask for another thing!"

Tracy glanced at the clock over Mrs. Bailey's head. Two-thirty-five. The first week of school was almost over. There had been lots of assignments during the week. Worksheets in math to see how much everyone had forgotten over the summer. A spelling list of words with matching definitions. Even a paragraph had been assigned titled, "Why a College Education Is

Important Today."

Tracy didn't turn any of the assignments in. She never even opened a book. She spent her time in class writing love letters and doodling *T.B.* + *R.A.* She never gave up the idea of getting into Mr. Arnold's class. So why bother doing work for Mrs. Bailey? It would just be thrown away when she switched classrooms.

"I have an important announcement to make," Mrs. Bailey said. "There's been a change in the science fair this year."

Tracy wasn't interested in the science fair. The only kids who made projects were straight *A* nerds.

"Those who participate can use their project for their science grade," Mrs. Bailey continued. "We've divided the fair into six categories. Each category has a supervising teacher."

Tracy stared at the clock's second hand and wondered how long she could hold her breath. She always spent the last five minutes of class trying to break her fourth-grade record. When she couldn't hold it anymore she blew the air out slowly. Sixty-three seconds. Anything over a minute was pretty good.

". . . and computers is Mr. Arnold," Mrs. Bailey said. "That's it."

For the first time in five days Mrs. Bailey had Tracy's attention. Tracy shot her hand up.

"Yes, Tracy?" Mrs. Bailey asked.

Tracy's face was red from holding her breath. "I missed the part about Mr. Arnold."

"Mr. Arnold is in charge of the computer projects."

Tracy looked puzzled.

Steve turned around in his seat. He blew peanut butter breath in Tracy's face. "For the science fair."

"Oh," Tracy said.

"Anyone interested can sign up after class," Mrs. Bailey said. "The first meeting is today at three."

This was the chance Tracy had been waiting for!

The dismissal bell rang and chairs skidded on the linoleum. Everyone scrambled for their books. Tracy took the half-eaten grilled cheese sandwich out of her backpack. She was waiting for everyone to leave. Then she'd sign up for Mr. Arnold's project.

"What're you waiting for?" Steve asked

Tracy wiped the grease off her chin. Then she ripped off a piece of crust and chomped. "Nothing."

"Don't tell me you're going to sign up for the fair?"

"Why not?" Tracy asked. "Everyone else in my family is a computer whiz. Maybe it's hereditary."

"But you'll have to stay after school every day."

"Yeah," Tracy sighed.

The classroom emptied in a hurry on Fridays. Tracy only noticed three kids stopping to sign up for the science fair. It was easy to imagine herself as Mr. Arnold's assistant. She'd wear an outfit like a nurse: a plain white dress, rubber-soled shoes, and thick panty hose.

Tracy stood up and headed for the front of the room. Steve was only a step behind.

"Oh, no, you don't, Steve Weber!" she stomped.

"Why not?" he asked. "It's better than reading that dumb science book."

Tracy quickly found the sheet of paper labeled "Computer Project" and signed her name. She decided the best way to deal with Steve was to ignore him. Mrs. Bailey was standing in the doorway, greeting the kids who'd signed up for "Rodent Project." Tracy flung her backpack over one shoulder and made a U-turn into Mr. Arnold's room. She slid into the front row center seat.

"We meet again," Mr. Arnold said, smiling.

Tracy thought she was going to melt. She flipped through the pages of her notebook looking for something to pretend to be reading until she got herself together. There was only one sheet of paper with writing on it. It started with *My dearest Mr. Arnold.* Tracy's cheeks flushed as she slammed her notebook shut.

Jill moved from her desk in the back of the room. She sat in the only empty chair next to Tracy. Steve was in the other one. "Isn't this great?!" she giggled.

"I think it stinks," Tracy whispered. "You have him all day long and after school, too. I thought I was going to get to work alone with him."

"Hey, Tracy?" Steve said, excitedly.

If looks were needles, Steve would have been the first human porcupine. "What is it now?!" She wanted to scream, Stop bugging me!

Steve hung his head. "It's nothing."

Mr. Arnold lifted a navy blue case to the top of his desk. It was about eighteen inches square and made out of lightweight material. The cover was held in place with strips of Velcro. Mr. Arnold ripped off the cover and pulled a small computer out of the case.

"Meet our computer," Mr. Arnold said.

Mr. Arnold then pulled out the keyboard. It reminded Tracy of a toy typewriter, only it didn't have a place for paper. He plugged the typewriter-thing into the computer-thing. Then he plugged both things into the wall.

Mr. Arnold held up a small control box. It had a gray cord tail.

Tracy couldn't wait to impress Mr. Arnold. "Isn't that a mouse?" she asked.

"I thought Mrs. Bailey was in charge of rodents," Steve said.

Even Tracy had to laugh at that one.

"Very good, Tracy," Mr. Arnold said. "Maybe I should put you in charge of the project." Tracy beamed. "Now, I have a manual for each of you," Mr. Arnold continued.

Mr. Arnold spent an hour explaining the basic principles of the computer. He even let them practice turning it on and off. Tracy liked the way the little happy face came on with a blinking question mark. She was going to read her manual backward and forward. If she couldn't be the only one working on Mr. Arnold's project, she'd be the best!

Then Mr. Arnold pulled out a portable cassette recorder. He held up a tape entitled "A Guided Tour of the Computer."

"Who'd like to go first?" Mr. Arnold asked.

All three kids waved their hands.

"I like your enthusiasm," Mr. Arnold said. "How about you Tracy? You seem to know something about our computer friend."

Tracy didn't really know a whole lot about computers. Sure, she'd tagged along with her sister to the University's computer lab. She'd seen a mouse used there. And sometimes she went to her dad's office and watched his secretary on the word processor. But that was about it.

Mr. Arnold held up a thin flat disk. One side had a shiny metal strip on it. "This is 'A Guided Tour' disk," he explained. "Okay, Tracy. Go ahead and put the disk in with the metal side up."

Tracy moved to Mr. Arnold's desk. She took the disk and stuck it in the skinny slot. The disk was swallowed up with a slurping sound.

"Wow!" Steve said. "I bet it hasn't eaten in a week."

Tracy laughed. Steve said some funny things for a fifth-grade boy.

Mr. Arnold turned on the tape recorder. The background music was a harp and a piano. Tracy would've liked it better if it was a rock song. But she wasn't complaining. She'd finally gotten into Mr. Arnold's room, even if it was only for a couple of hours a day.

"This is the guided tour of the computer," a man's voice crackled through the speaker.

Tracy listened carefully. The first exercise was called "My Friend, the Mouse." She followed the instructions and pushed the mouse across the top of Mr. Arnold's desk. When she moved it in a circle, the little arrow on the screen moved in a circle. When she moved it in a straight line, that's how the arrow moved.

"Hey, this is easy!" Tracy was excited.

Mr. Arnold patted the top of Tracy's head. "You're doing a great job."

I'll never wash my hair again! Tracy thought.

Nine

TRACY spent the entire weekend with her nose buried in her computer manual. She studied mouse techniques during the commercials on Saturday's cartoons. She studied how to open and close the computer's files between waffles on Sunday. She even turned down roller-skating with Jill to memorize how the computer's keyboard worked.

Tracy was sitting cross-legged on the living room couch. The computer manual was open and resting in her lap. She was wearing the same pj's she'd changed into Friday night. There wasn't any reason to get dressed. She wasn't going anywhere until she'd memorized the menus under every menu bar.

Tracy turned on her new pocket calculator and pushed the print button. "If there are five days in a school week," she muttered to herself, "and one-and-a-half hours after school every day working with the computer . . . ." She pushed the numbers, then locked them into the memory. "And three people who want equal time on the computer . . . ."

"My sister the bookworm," Kristina teased. She was in her Sunday clothes: dirty old sweats with paint stains.

"Look at the puzzle icon," Tracy said, excitedly. She held up the manual and pointed to the picture of a puzzle. There were fifteen numbers and one blank in four rows. The object was to use the mouse to move the numbers until they were in order. "Computers are better than video games."

"This Mr. Arnold must really be something," she said.

Tracy didn't like the tone of her sister's voice.

"What're you talking about?"

"Do you think I just fell off the turnip truck?" Kristina asked. Then she slid over the back of the couch. "I had a crush on a teacher once—Mr. Purwin. I used to sharpen his pencils down to the erasers."

Mrs. Benedict rounded the corner of the living room and dumped an arm full of clothes next to Tracy. "What're you two up to?" she asked.

"We were just discussing bow-wow love," Kristina said.

Tracy wanted to kick her sister in the shin. "It is NOT puppy love."

"Then what is it?" Kristina asked.

"It's . . . it's . . . it's none of your business!"

Curls were pulled up into a knot on top of her mom's head. Frizzy little ringlets framed her face and hung down the back of her neck. She shook out a pair of jeans and folded them.

"I remember the first time I met your dad," her mom said. "It was love at first sight."

Her dad had only been gone for a week.

Already Tracy was having a hard time remembering what he looked like. She liked the mustache he grew on the last trip. It tickled her cheek when he kissed her. What if he came home with a beard the next time? She might not recognize him.

"Was it mutual?" Kristina asked.

"Nah." Her mom smiled. "He played hard to get."

Tracy grabbed a bunch of socks and started pairing them. She never got tired of hearing stories about her parents. She wished her dad sold shoes or was a checker in the grocery store. She didn't even care how much money he made. She just wanted him to stay home.

"How did you finally win him over?" Tracy asked.

"I wouldn't take no for an answer," Mrs. Benedict said.

Tracy was happy that the plan had worked. Otherwise she might've ended up with some stranger for a father. She was also happy because it was the same plan she was using on Mr. Arnold. And she had every reason to believe things would turn out the same for her as they had for her mom.

When it was time for bed Tracy put the "Guided Tour" tape into her cassette. She thought if she listened to the tape while she slept her brain would record everything. And even though she didn't have her own computer to practice on, she could use what she learned to impress Mr. Arnold.

The last thing she remembered was the man's voice trailing off, "Show me my electronic . . ."

The next thing she heard was, "Tracy, wake up." It was her mom. "Your alarm didn't go off."

Tracy sat up and looked at her clock radio. She only had five minutes to get dressed and grab something to eat. She couldn't be late. A tardy meant a detention. A detention meant she'd be in the principal's office after school. Then she wouldn't be in Mr. Arnold's room for the computer meeting.

Tracy never got dressed so fast in her life. She didn't even care that the blouse she pulled out from under the bed was wrinkled. She tossed the computer manual in her backpack along with the cassette tape.

Three minutes later Tracy was racing down the hall. "I'm ready!"

"I'll butter some toast," her mom said. She pushed the toaster lever down. "You can eat it in the car."

It wouldn't take long to get to school since they were going in the family station wagon and her mom didn't have to shift gears. Tracy was chewing on the last piece of crust when they pulled into the school's loading zone.

Jill was leaning on the bike rack. She flicked nuts off the end of her finger from her cinnamon roll. "I have good news," she hollered while Tracy was getting out of the car. "And I have bad news. Which one do you want to hear first?"

Tracy slammed the car door with a good-bye to her mom. She didn't like the sound of bad news.

"This doesn't have anything to do with Mr. Arnold, does it?"

Jill licked her sticky fingers. "Yup."

Tracy couldn't stand the suspense. "Give me the bad news first."

"Mr. Arnold wants us to spend our lunch hours working on the project."

"That's bad news?" Tracy said. "I think that's great!"

Jill ripped off a piece of her roll. She held it out to Tracy. "You wouldn't think it was so great if you were in his room," Jill said. "His idea of fun is a worksheet of word problems. Just like a teacher."

"Then why don't you trade classes with me?"

Jill shook her head. "No way."

"Why not? You just said . . . "

"Because," Jill stopped her. She nodded toward the basketball court. Steve and Mark were shooting baskets. "I'm going to stick with someone my own age."

Tracy couldn't believe that her best friend

would fall for a fifth-grade nerd. "Not Steve Weber!"

"No," Jill said. "I sit behind Mark Byrd. He's really neat, Tracy. We went roller-skating yesterday afternoon. Besides, if you changed classrooms you'd be breaking someone's heart."

"What're you talking about?"

"Tracy and Steve," Jill sang. "Sitting in a tree. K-I-S-S-I-N-G!"

"Ugh!" Tracy made a face. "Not in a million years!"

The first bell rang and everyone scattered for their classrooms. Tracy and Jill rounded the corner of the hallway to find Mr. Arnold standing outside of his door. He was wearing a navy blue tie with little red dots on it. Tracy didn't understand how Jill could change her mind about Mr. Arnold. The more Tracy saw of him the more she knew she was in love. It wasn't puppy love, either. It was the real thing!

"Good morning, Tracy," Mr. Arnold said. He stepped sideways to open the door for her. "Did you have a nice weekend?"

Tracy couldn't believe that Mr. Arnold was opening the door for her. It was a big deal if one of Kristina's dates opened a car door. That's how they earned brownie points.

"Will we have a chance to play with the puzzle icon today?" Tracy asked.

"An *icon*?" Mr. Arnold was impressed with Tracy's use of the word.

"What's an icon?" Jill asked.

"Icons are the little pictures that appear on the computer screen," Tracy said. "They represent different things stored in the computer. The puzzle icon looks like a picture of a puzzle. There are also icons of an alarm clock, a calculator, a clipboard, a note pad, and a scrapbook." Tracy was going to use computer lingo every chance she got.

"Did you get the message about the noon meeting?" Mr. Arnold asked.

"Uh-huh," Tracy answered. Then she corrected herself with, "Yes, sir."

Tracy had already figured out why Mr. Arnold wanted a lunch meeting. It was so they could spend more time together.

"See you at twelve," Mr. Arnold said. Then he disappeared into his classroom.

"You won't see me," Jill piped up. "I'm quitting the project."

"Why?" Tracy was surprised.

"If I'm going to spend that much time on science I oughta get an *A* for the rest of my life, not just one lousy report card! Besides, I'm meeting Mark at the cafeteria. Today's hot dog day."

One down and one to go, Tracy thought.

Now all Tracy had to do was think of a way to get rid of Steve. Then she'd have Mr. Arnold all to herself!

Ten

TRACY took a peanut butter sandwich out of a baggy. She set it on top of her desk. Steve had tuna fish on whole wheat oozing with mayonnaise and relish.

"Do you want to swap halves?" Steve asked.

Tracy just gave Steve an impatient look and shook her head.

Three weeks had gone by since Jill quit the computer project but Tracy still hadn't gotten rid of Steve Weber. He reminded Tracy of a giant pimple that showed up one morning and never went away. Then after a couple of weeks, she'd gotten used to looking at it.

Tracy and Steve decided on a treasure hunt for

their project. They'd learned how to use the computer's drawing program. By clicking the mouse they could make all kinds of lines and patterns. There was a pencil icon for skinny lines and a paintbrush icon for thick lines. There was even a picture of an eraser for mistakes. Tracy's favorite was the can of spray paint for drawing graffiti.

They used the drawing program to draw a map for hunting for the treasure chest. There were lots of arrows and little signs. Tracy drew a small treasure chest next to the X in the center of the map. Steve added a skull and crossbones. There were lots of squiggly marks that didn't mean anything. They were added to confuse the hunters.

Tracy and Steve used the computer to write clues for their treasure hunt. The plan was to hand out copies of the clues on a map on the night of the science fair. The person who found the treasure chest would get to keep it. It was a shoe box full of markers and funny stickers.

Tracy took the shoe box home two days before the fair. She dunked strips of newspaper into a bowl of water mixed with glue and brown shoe polish. Then she covered the box to make it look like a real treasure chest. It was Steve's idea to collect soft drink bottles from the trash cans at school. They glued the broken glass inside the top. When they were finished the shoe box looked like a treasure chest full of jewels.

Tracy held up the box for Mr. Arnold to see. "What do you think?" she asked.

Mr. Arnold smiled. "What a team!"

Tracy grinned. She always knew that she and Mr. Arnold would make a good team. Now Mr. Arnold thought so, too!

Steve and Tracy spent the following afternoon getting the kinks out of their project. Mr. Arnold brought the printer to school and hooked it up to the computer. They were excited to see what their treasure map looked like on paper. So far they'd only seen it on the computer's screen.

Tracy had the honor of pulling the first map

out of the printer. "Wow!" she exclaimed. "Do you think our project will win first prize?"

First prize was a giant blue ribbon. It was made out of satin and SCIENCE FAIR was printed across the middle in gold letters. The ribbon was hanging in a glass case inside the administration office. Tracy looked at it every day before school.

Steve eyed the map over Tracy's shoulder. "Do you really think we have a chance?"

Mr. Arnold turned the computer off. "I don't know anyone who has worked harder on their project than you two," he said. "And I'm behind you one hundred percent."

Tracy had a curling iron and the clothes she was going to wear to the fair in a grocery bag under her school chair. It wasn't easy talking her mom into letting her stay at school until the fair started at six o'clock. Tracy knew there wouldn't be a lot of time between their meeting and fair time. She also knew that if she went home her mom would make her eat something. Tracy was too nervous to eat.

Mr. Arnold glanced at the clock. "It's already five o'clock," he said. "I'll meet you two on stage at six sharp. No matter what happens, your project is something to be proud of."

Tracy was proud of it, too. "Thanks," she said.

Mrs. Benedict had taken Tracy shopping earlier in the week. Tracy wanted a pair of dark blue pants and a pretty blue, fuzzy sweater for the fair. Her mom thought a skirt would be more appropriate, but Tracy didn't want anyone to see her hairy legs. Her mom finally gave in.

Tracy was changing clothes in the girls' bathroom when Jill walked in. "Your sweater is out-a-sight!" Jill said.

"What took you so long?" Tracy asked. "My curling iron's been hot for half-an-hour."

"I stopped by the auditorium to check things out," she said. "I don't know why you can't tell me what your project is."

"Because it's a secret," Tracy said. "Did you see my mom?"

"Nah, but I saw your sister. I think your mom was parking the car." Jill took a strand of Tracy's hair. "How do you want it?"

"Let's curl it all over," Tracy answered. She took a couple of bobby pins out of her bag. "I want it like my mom's when it's pinned up on top of her head."

Jill even curled Tracy's bangs. "It looks great," Jill said. "You're going to knock 'em dead."

Tracy stood back to admire herself in the mirror. "Do you think Mr. Arnold will like it?"

Jill rolled her eyeballs. Tracy knew she was sick and tired of hearing about Mr. Arnold. "He got so excited about your project that he's making us study that dumb computer during class time. It's boring!"

"It's not boring," Tracy said. "It's fun. Besides, Mr. Arnold said he's going to ask Mrs. Bailey if I can come over half-an-hour a day to help. How can she say no when it's in the name of science?"

Tracy wadded her school clothes into a ball and stuffed them into the grocery bag. There was something else in the bottom of the bag. A secret that even Jill didn't know about. It was a card and envelope that she'd bought at the dime store. On the outside of the card were two love birds. There wasn't anything printed on the inside. That's where Tracy put her message.

Tracy got the idea to give Mr. Arnold a card the day he called them a team. The best team Tracy could imagine was husband and wife. Who says the guy has to be the one who proposes? It's the twentieth century. If Kristina could ask a guy to the movies, Tracy could ask Mr. Arnold to marry her.

Tracy and Jill entered the auditorium from backstage. The curtain was closed. All of the science projects were set up on card tables in a semicircle across the stage. Mrs. Bailey was standing next to the table with a mouse maze. The maze was made out of popsicle sticks and was painted to look like the front on their school. The mice rang a miniature school bell to get their food.

Tracy peeked through the curtains. "I see Kristina," she said. "But where's my mom? It can't take that long to park a car. Gads, you don't suppose she forgot?"

"No way," Jill said. Then she punched Tracy in the shoulder. "Break a leg. I'm going to find a seat out front."

Jill slipped through the curtains and disappeared. Tracy was getting nervous. She felt like there were bats **dive**-bombing in her stomach. Steve, also wearing new clothes, was standing next to the card table with the computer. He had on a plaid shirt and brown cords, sort of a preppie look.

"Did you hear?" Steve asked. "They're going to pin the ribbons on the projects before opening the curtains."

Tracy thought it was a stupid idea. "Why? It'll ruin the suspense."

Steve squirted window cleaner on the computer's screen and wiped it clean. Tracy thought he treated the computer like a human

being. "They only have time to demonstrate the top three projects and two of the runners-up," he said.

Tracy looked around at all of the tables and all of the projects. Everyone had worked so hard. It wasn't fair that some of the kids wouldn't get a chance to show what they'd done. Suddenly she wasn't as worried about winning the blue ribbon as she was being a runner-up.

Mr. Arnold walked over. "And how are the computer whizzes?"

"Nervous," Tracy said. "Have you heard the verdict?"

Mr. Arnold patted Tracy's shoulder before he walked away.

The principal stepped up to the microphone and tapped it with his finger. "Testing one, two." Then he turned to Mrs. Bailey and told her to proceed.

Mrs. Bailey was in charge of the ribbons. She taped the first runner's-up ribbon to the leg of the card table with a smoking volcano. The second runner's-up ribbon went to a plastic model of the human body. It had a flashing red Christmas tree light as a heart. She hooked the third place ribbon over the popsicle stick maze. Then she scratched the top of the mouse's head, "Congratulations."

Tracy was thinking about her mom and sister in the audience waiting for the treasure chest map. "What if we don't get a ribbon?" she asked.

Mr. Arnold winked. "Don't worry."

Mrs. Bailey only had two ribbons left. The only difference between the first and second prizes was the color of the ribbon. They were both the same size: BIG!

Mrs. Bailey stopped in front of their card table. "Sorry," she said to Tracy and Steve. "I really thought you'd get first prize." Then she stuck the shiny red ribbon to the computer's screen.

"Second prize!" Mr. Arnold said. "That's super!"

Mr. Arnold shook Steve's hand, then gave Tracy a hug. Tracy couldn't think of a better time to give Mr. Arnold the envelope.

Suddenly a woman rushed up from behind. Tracy had never seen her before.

"Congratulations, darling!" the woman squealed.

Mr. Arnold stood up. He put his arm around the woman's waist and kissed her on the cheek. Tracy didn't know who she was, but she wanted her to keep her hands off Mr. Arnold.

"Meet the real pros," Mr. Arnold said. "This is Tracy Benedict. And Steve Weber. Tracy, Steve, meet my fianceé, Valerie Crawford."

Eleven

"OPEN that door!" Steve pounded on the cloak room.

Tracy wiped her cheeks with the sleeve of someone's coat. It smelled like moth balls.

"You're acting like a spoiled brat!" Steve shouted. "Just because you didn't win first prize. I worked just as hard on the project as you did. You don't see me locking myself in the closet."

Tracy put the wool sleeve in her mouth. She bit down as hard as she could. She wanted to scream and shout at the top of her lungs. And to think she was just getting ready to ask Mr. Arnold to marry her when he'd asked someone else! She felt like such a jerk. A class A number

one jerk!

"I'm not coming out," Tracy sobbed. "And no one can make me."

"I saw your mom when I handed out the maps." Steve was trying a new strategy. "She said she has a surprise for you."

Tracy couldn't take any more surprises.

"Come on, Tracy." Now Steve was pleading.

"It won't be any fun without you."

Tracy cracked the door. A big black hat fell off the top shelf of the closet. She put it on and pulled the rim down over her forehead, hoping it would hide her eyes. She didn't want anyone to know that she'd been crying.

Steve led Tracy to the stage. The curtain was open and the stage was bright with spotlights. They stood next to the computer while the principal thanked the parents for coming. Tracy had missed the entire presentation. She didn't know how she could've been so stupid to fall for Mr. Arnold. Heck, he seemed almost old enough to be her father!

All of the parents were milling around looking at their kids' projects. "Tracy!" Her mom rushed across stage. "We're so proud of you!"

"Where's this Mr. Arnold?" Kristina asked. "I can't wait to meet him."

Steve pointed to Mr. Arnold. He was standing in the wings holding hands with his fianceé.

"He looks a lot like your dad, Tracy," her mom

said. "A lot younger, of course, and without a mustache."

"Wait'll I tell him what I read in Tracy's diary," Kristina teased. "Look, he's coming this way."

It was times like this that Tracy wished she was an only child. Or had never been born. How was she going to face Mr. Arnold? And what was she going to say to him? "Why is that woman wearing the engagement ring that belongs on my finger?"

Mr. Arnold introduced himself to Mrs. Benedict. "You must be very proud of your daughter," he said.

"I'm not the only one," she answered.

Tracy didn't know what her mother meant. She couldn't think of anyone else who would be proud of her.

Then her dad stepped out from behind the curtain. "I'm proud of you, too, Peanuts."

"Daddy!" Tracy squealed. She threw her arms around her father's neck. "When did you get home?"

Her dad returned the hug. "I flew in this afternoon."

"Maybe you'd like to be the first one to see this," Mr. Arnold said. He handed Mr. Benedict an envelope. "It's Tracy's grade card for the first quarter."

Mr. Benedict opened the envelope and read Tracy's grade out loud. "An *A* in science?" At first he sounded surprised. Then he said, "I knew you could do it!"

"An *A*?" Tracy couldn't believe it. She stared at the grade card. "I really got an *A*?"

"You earned it," Mr. Arnold said.

Mr. Benedict put his arm around Tracy's shoulders. "What do you say we celebrate over a pizza?"

Tracy's stomach growled and she knew she was on the road to recovery. "Pepperoni and olives!"

Tracy hooked her arm through her dad's elbow. Together, they trotted through the auditorium. Mrs. Benedict and Kristina were one step behind.

Tracy stopped when they reached the front door. "Wait a minute," she said. "There's something I forgot to do."

"Okay," her father said. "But don't be long. I'll get the car."

Tracy raced through the auditorium and up the steps to the stage. She'd forgotten to say good-bye to Mr. Arnold. The funny part was that it didn't seem to matter now. Instead, she looked for Steve. He was wrapping the mouse cord in a neat figure eight.

"I almost forgot." Tracy huffed out of breath. "Who found the treasure chest?"

"Jill and Mark teamed up," Steve said. "It only took them five minutes."

"Oh." Tracy didn't know what else to say.

She wanted to tell Steve that he wasn't so bad after all. At least not for a fifth-grade boy. And that he'd been an okay partner on their project. She also wanted to thank him for talking her out of the closet. She didn't know what would've happened if her dad had found her there.

"You want to keep the ribbon?" Tracy asked. "For the first week?"

Steve accepted eagerly. "Gee, thanks," he said.

Tracy patted the computer. "I guess I'll see you both tomorrow."

"Okay," Steve said, grinning. "See ya."

About the Author

SHERRY SHAHAN is married and has two daughters. She and her family live on a horse ranch called Hidden Oaks in California where they breed and raise racehorses. Sherry considers herself an "adventurer at heart." Every year, she and her husband take a special trip to a foreign land and explore the countryside on horseback. They have traveled across Argentina, Kenya, New Zealand, and Hawaii on horses.

Sherry has been a writer for ten years. She gets her inspiration from everyday life with her own children. She also writes articles about her travels for magazines.

When Sherry is not busy writing or chauffeuring her children, she enjoys aerobics, jogging, and bicycling.